FOR GIRLY from MARGARET

PLEASE don't torment Tootsie

by Margaret Chamberlain

First published in hardback in 2008
by Hodder Children's Books

Copyright © Margaret Chamberlain 2008

Hodder Children's Books
338 Euston Road
London NW1 3BH

Hodder Children's Books Australia
Level 17/207 Kent Street
Sydney, NSW 2000

The right of Margaret Chamberlain
to be identified as the author and illustrator
of this Work has been asserted by her in accordance
with the Copyright, Designs and Patents Act 1988.

ISBN: 978 0 340 93241 4

Printed in China

Hodder Children's Books is a division of Hachette Children's Books.
An Hachette Livre UK Company.

PLEASE

don't torment Tootsie

Margaret Chamberlain

Hodder Children's Books

A division of Hachette Children's Books

PLEASE

don't torment
Tootsie,

or provoke
Poochie.

Don't madden
Mutley,

or disturb Dixi.

Do not bully Bitsy,

or even think
of teasing Trixi.

You'd be MAD

to wind up Whitney.

Just give her
a little pat...

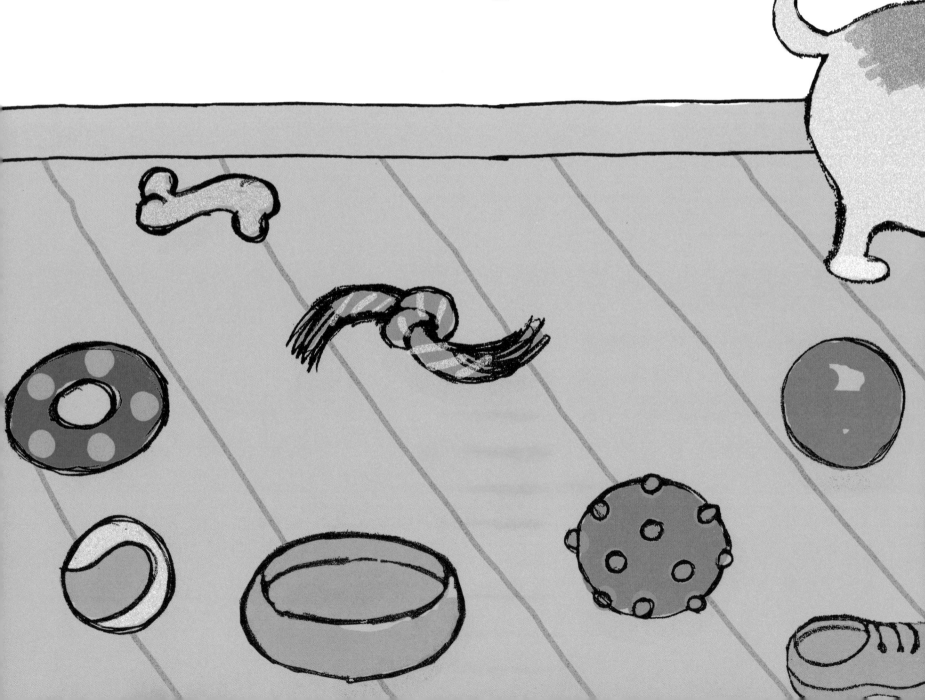

Dixie cat.

Mutley's here for you
to dote on.
Will you put his new
blue coat on?

For
Mutley

Trixi needs
a special treat.

How about
a green newt sweet?

It's Bitsy's day
for bunny fun,

so MAKE THE EFFORT

EVERYONE!

Calm down,
Poochie.
It's all right,
she's gone.

Poor Tootsie!
Pretty Tootsie!
Come and curl up
on your mat.

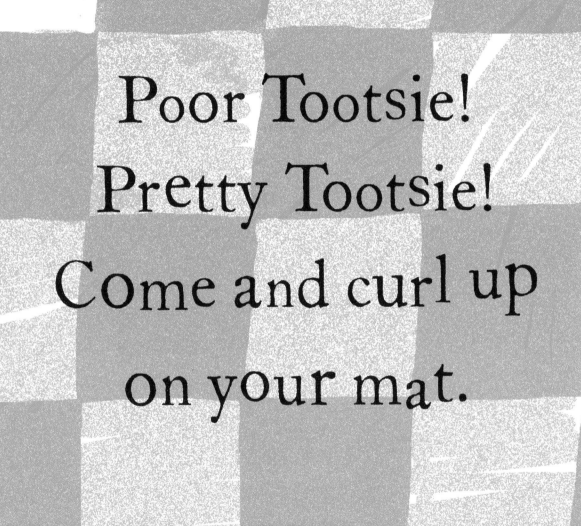

We will stroke you,
never poke you.

We love you,
TOOTSIE CAT!